or
SHALL WE
DIE?

IAN McEWAN

or
SHALL WE DIE?

*Words for an oratorio
set to music by
Michael Berkeley*

JONATHAN CAPE
THIRTY BEDFORD SQUARE
LONDON

FIRST PUBLISHED 1983
COPYRIGHT © BY IAN MCEWAN 1983
JONATHAN CAPE LTD,
30 BEDFORD SQUARE, LONDON WC1

BRITISH LIBRARY CATALOGUING
IN PUBLICATION DATA

MCEWAN, IAN
OR SHALL WE DIE?
I. ATOMIC WARFARE
I. TITLE
355'.0217   UF767

ISBN 0–224–02947–9

Note

Or Shall We Die? was commissioned from Ian McEwan and Michael Berkeley by the London Symphony Orchestra Chorus with funds provided by the Arts Council of Great Britain. It was first performed at the Royal Festival Hall on 6 February 1983 by Heather Harper (Soprano) and Stephen Roberts (Baritone) and the London Symphony Orchestra and Chorus conducted by Richard Hickox.

TYPESET BY GLOUCESTER TYPESETTING SERVICES
PRINTED IN GREAT BRITAIN BY
NEW WESTERN PRINTING LTD, BRISTOL

For Polly and Alice
and all children

INTRODUCTION

THE SUBJECT MATTER of this oratorio seemed more of an inevitability than a choice. Throughout 1980, along with many others, I found myself disturbed and obsessed by the prospect of a new and madly vigorous arms race. Russia had recently invaded Afghanistan and later in the year there was the possibility of intervention in Poland. In the United States public opinion, or media opinion – the two are sometimes hard to separate – was demanding a restoration of American might after the perceived humiliation of the Iranian hostage crisis, and by the end of the year a new president had been elected who promised a programme of weapon manufacture on a scale without precedent. In this country the government was committed to increasing and 'improving' our nuclear capability. The Russians meanwhile were steadily deploying their SS 20 missiles. The language of the nuclear apologists had taken a fresh turn: there was open talk of a limited and winnable nuclear war in which Europe would serve as a battleground for the two major powers. Weapons had been devised accordingly. The fragile concept of deterrence had been shaken by the determination on both sides to find ever more accurate missiles that could hit enemy silos – weapons that were only of use in a first strike, before the enemy could empty its silos.

One turned in vain to the history books to discover a time when nations prepared so extensively for war and none had happened. And yet between East and West there were no obvious territorial disputes. Despite scare stories to the contrary, there was no ruthless competition for diminishing resources. And the extent of the mutual dependence for new markets and new technology was so great as to undermine any pretence of a genuine ideological conflict. It was as if each side prepared for war because it saw the other doing the same. The governments of each side had much in common, as did their civilian populations who were united by the prospect of annihilation and – in attitude – by their indifference, or by their helplessness and fear. For all the complex discussion of nuclear strategy with its unique blend of logic and paranoia, at heart the situation had about it the aspect of very simple human folly. To call it childish would be to demean children, who would soon tire of such a game: I'm getting ready to hit you because you are getting ready to hit me. That this madness, which threatens not only human life, present and future, but all life on the planet, should be presented on our television screens as sanity, as responsible deliberation on 'defence' policy by calm, authoritative men in suits, gave the matter the quality of a nightmare; either they were completely mad, or we were. Ultimately, however, I believe their madness is ours, and the responsibility for survival is a collective one.

The widespread apprehension experienced in 1980 brought about large-scale public opposition in Europe and later in the United States. Now three-quarters of all Americans appear to favour some form of freeze on weapon construction, and peace movements can claim to have modified, at least, the rhetoric of politicians. For all that, the arms race continues. New weapon systems are to be introduced across Europe during 1983, and the Russians have continued to deploy their medium-range missiles. Public opposition has had only minimal effect on policy, but its importance is greater than its effect – that opposition represents all the hope there is.

Public opposition, of course, had its roots in private fears, and in 1980 I was struck by how deeply the lives of individuals had been shaken by the new cold war. It was precisely this that made me want to write about it. Those who were parents, or had children in their lives, seemed particularly affected. Love of children generates a fierce ambition for the world to continue and be safe, and makes one painfully vulnerable to fantasies of loss. Like others, I experienced the jolt of panic that wakes you before dawn, the daydreams of the mad rush of people and cars out of the city before it is destroyed, of losing a child in the confusion. People described the pointlessness of planning ahead, a creeping sense of the irrelevance of all the things they valued against the threat of annihilation. Helplessness generated anger, which in turn threatened friendships. Images of nuclear war invaded dreams. As in war itself, matters of public policy had profound consequences for private lives.

For most people the panic could not last. A kind of numbness descends, and we have a saving – or is it fatal? – ability to compartmentalise, to keep dread in one room, hope or indifference in another. The threat remains, we continue to deplore it, a few of us take action, but life goes on, thankfully, and most of us learn to sleep again without nightmares.

I wanted to write about those private fears while they were still fresh. I thought the subject matter was best suited to film. I wrote outlines and abandoned them. I sketched out the opening chapters of a novel – but in all these attempts I felt defeated by scale; the problem was at once so colossal and so human. How could it be made to fit? And yet as soon as Michael Berkeley asked me to consider writing a libretto for an oratorio, I felt certain that this could be a way of approaching the subject. Music would at once translate it to another realm, abstract, beyond definitions, and yet with direct appeal to feelings. Michael Berkeley's music, and especially his oboe concerto, had affected me enormously: though its textures and complexities were undeniably contemporary, his was also an accessible music, often rhythmically exciting, with expressive melodies. His music had the power to move. He belonged to a tradition of English composers who have drawn inspiration from their country's literature. He had written settings of poems by Donne, Herbert, Lewis Carroll and Hardy, among others, and had composed a particularly beautiful piece for piano inspired by Wilfred Owen's poem 'Strange Meeting'. Above all, it turned out that he shared my feelings about the urgency of the subject matter. He introduced me to Tippett's oratorio *A Child of Our Time*, written in the thirties when another war in Europe was a growing possibility. The Mother in this work certainly influenced the presence of the mother in my libretto.

One immediate attraction of an oratorio was purely formal; a man's voice set against a woman's, and both set against a choir, addressing a matter of moral and spiritual crisis by singing about it directly, without the complications of a dramatic setting, and in terms that could be alternately public or intimate – there was a purity about this that was appealing. No characters, no psychology, no actors pretending to be other people, simply voices articulating profoundest fears and some hope. There was too the challenge, as I saw it, of writing a singable English, simple and clear, that could express public themes without pomposity and private feelings without bathos. As it turned out, *Or Shall We Die?* took on a certain amount of dramatic shape since the voices assume a number of different roles, though these are not sufficiently defined to be characters. And whether the oratorio's language is clear or singable will not be discovered until the first performance, which is still some months ahead as I write.

Traditionally, an oratorio is a non-dramatic choral work that addresses a religious theme. Clearly it could be extended to include moral, political or even private themes, and there is, in fact, a well-established secular tradition. The oratorio, rather like the novel, is more a term of convenience than of precise definition. To present at the beginning of this secular oratorio the idea of a mother and child may seem a deliberate and even too obvious an invocation of the form's religious tradition. Tippett was an influence, but often it is only in retrospect that one realises how one's choices may be influenced by a particular work one admires, and powerfully shaped by archetypal forms. At the time of writing I thought of the woman who sings the first section as an exact contemporary of mine, someone I might know well – a woman not necessarily given to millennial thoughts, who delights in a clear summer's evening and remembers, precisely at the moment of her greatest joy, the threat of war.

She may have heard of or read accounts of the bombing of Hiroshima. Mrs Tomoyasu was a young woman in 1945 whose nine-year-old daughter died in her arms. She told her story to Jonathan Dimbleby in his film *In Evidence: the Bomb* and I am indebted to him, and to Mrs Tomoyasu and to Yorkshire Television, for the use of her words – changed only to make smoother rhythms – in section five. Although Mrs Tomoyasu's terrible experience is almost forty years in the past, I thought of it as a ghostly prefiguration in section one, the starkest embodiment of what we most fear from nuclear strategy.

During the time I spent considering exactly how the oratorio should proceed, I speculated that if there was intelligent life elsewhere in the universe, it was likely that sooner or later it would discover that matter and energy are not distinct entities but lie along a continuum. For civilisations without high technology the discovery would pose no threat. Long before Einstein's theories, the Chinese term for physics was *Wu Li*, in which the word *Wu* can mean either matter or energy. The identification of the two has long been a feature of eastern religions. In the Mundaka Upanishad it says: 'By energism of consciousness, Brahman is massed; from that Matter is born and from Matter, Life, Mind and the Worlds.' For those civilisations with technology, on the other hand, the means for total self-destruction would become available. It is as if nuclear energy is a kind of evolutionary filter, and this is the argument of the second section. Of those civilisations who make the discovery, only those who do not build the weapons or, less likely, build them and do not use them, survive to evolve further.

Later I discovered that this speculation of mine was at least as old as nuclear weapons. I heard one scientist fantasise about speeding time up to such an extent that one could look out across the universe and see countless pinprick flares of intelligent civilisations destroying themselves because their cleverness had outrun their wisdom.

From this remote perspective, the existence of nuclear weapons not only threatens but also indicts us all. It is not simply a matter of what governments do to us, but of what we are, and what we could become. If there is to be no nuclear war it will be because a sufficient number of people, inside and outside governments, set about securing this end. In the final resort the responsibility is for the species as a whole. If our evolutionary test defeats us, it will defeat us all.

The first nuclear weapons were developed in the early 1940s and built for use against the Germans. By the time the first bombs were ready, Germany had surrendered and instead the inhabitants of Hiroshima and Nagasaki became the first victims of nuclear attack. It was by no means an inevitable choice. Reading the minutes of the committees set up to advise the American President on the use of the bomb, and reading the accounts of the deliberations of various interested groups, I was surprised by the extent of the opposition to the use of the bomb against civilians, and by the humanity and far-sightedness of the arguments deployed. There were numerous proposals; dropping the bomb in the desert or the ocean with Japanese observers present was one line of approach, discounted for many reasons. The US Navy was convinced that a blockade would bring a Japanese surrender within months. Japan's industrial output was a fraction of its pre-war figure, and raw materials were virtually non-existent. There was one forcefully argued case for dropping the bomb on a huge forest of cryptomeria trees not far from Tokyo. The trees would be felled along the line of blast, and the power of a single bomb would be evident. Beyond all this, intercepted and deciphered radio traffic suggested that powerful figures in the Japanese military, with access to the Emperor, were convinced that Japan could not win the war and were seeking a surrender – albeit a conditional surrender that would salvage some degree of national dignity. There were those in the US adminis-tration who argued that in this instance the difference between conditional and unconditional surrender was little more than verbal, and that with some flexibility the war could be ended by diplomatic means.

However, the bomb seemed to have had its own momentum. It was a triumph of theoretical and techno-logical daring. The scientists working on the project were so involved in solving countless problems, and so elated when they succeeded, that many of them lost touch with the ultimate goal of their labours – colossal destruction. The bomb was a pinnacle of human achieve-ment – intellect divorced from feeling – and there appears to have been a deep, collective desire to see it used, despite all arguments. Opponents of its use were always on the defensive. Furthermore, at the beginning of the war, genocide had been the strategy of the Axis powers alone. By 1945 it had become acceptable to all combatants; fascism had to be defeated by fascism's methods, and the mass destruction at Hiroshima and Nagasaki had powerful precedents in the fire bombing of Dresden and Tokyo.

The nuclear bombing of these two cities, then, was not purely the responsibility of a handful of genocidally inclined military advisers; it was made possible by a general state of mind, by a deep fascination with technological solutions, by judgments barbarised by warfare and by nations which – rightly or wrongly – had organised themselves to inflict destruction. The public, when it heard the news of the bombing, though shocked was by no means overwhelmingly critical. Ever since that time, attempts to prevent the proliferation of nuclear weapons have been a total failure. There are now more than sixty thousand nuclear warheads, primed and programmed for their destinations. The smaller of these are vastly more powerful than the Hiroshima bomb. If, as a species, we faced a simple test of wisdom, from the very outset we appeared to be intent on failure.

Before the slaughter there never seems to be a priest lacking to bless the executioners. The chorus's lines in section three reflect my conviction that whatever moral or spiritual resources are necessary for us to avoid destroying ourselves they are unlikely to be provided by the world-weary bureaucracies of the established churches, nor by any religious sect that claims that it alone has the ear of God. If, for example, the Church of England comes to accept, as is likely, the idea that within women as well as men there is a spiritual dimension that could enable them to become priests, it will be less from conviction than from tired capitulation to changes in the secular world. In the same way, the Church may follow the opposition to militarism but never – as an institution – lead it. This is not to deny, of course, that many exceptional individuals work within that and other churches. But centuries of mind-numbing dogma, professionalisation and enmeshment in privilege have all but annihilated the mystical and spiritual experience that is said to be at the heart of Christianity.

During the first thirty years of this century there occurred a scientific revolution whose significance we are only now beginning to understand, for its repercussions are not confined to science. Space, time, matter, energy, light, all came to be thought of in entirely new ways, and ultimately must affect the way we see the world and our place within it. We continue, of course, to live within a Newtonian universe – its physics are perfectly adequate to describe and measure the world we can see; only the very large and the very small are beyond its grasp. More importantly, our habits of mind, our intellectual and moral frameworks, are consonant with the Newtonian world-view. The impartial observer of Newtonian thought is so pervasive a presence in all our thinking that it is difficult to describe this 'commonsense' world in anything but its terms. Detachment is a characteristic we value highly in intellectual activity, so too is objectivity. In our medicine we describe the human personality as a static structure (superego, ego, id) and the body as a vastly complicated clock whose individual parts can be treated in isolation when they fail. We conceive of ourselves moving through time in an orderly, linear fashion in which cause invariably precedes effect. When it appears not to, as in, say, a precognitive dream, we are quick to dismiss the experience, or ridicule as superstitious those who do not. We frequently describe the world as though we ourselves were invisible. Environments are planned – from tower blocks to new social orders – as though people en masse are utterly distinct from the planners, and can be acted upon and shaped like clay. Though we recognise the line of our descent, for the most part we consider other animals as little more than automata to be experimented on or destroyed as we require. We stand separate from our world – and from ourselves and from each other – describing, measuring, shaping it like gods.

The insufficiency of this paradigm – knowledge as 'mastery' of the unknown – is expressed in the final section and in section four a kind of battle hymn celebrates ironically the most aggressive form of this world-view. Logic, discipline, objectivity, thought unmuddied by emotion, are qualities traditionally associated with the male, and patriarchal values are celebrated here in the same manner. Because governments have never sought public opinion on nuclear policy until after that policy has been shaped, and because of the cult of secrecy that surrounds them, nuclear weapons are represented here as powerfully subversive of democratic procedures.

Only when I had finished a first draft of the libretto did it occur to me to insert the stanzas from William Blake's 'The Tyger', 'A Divine Image', and 'The Divine Image'. This particularly pleased Michael Berkeley whose piece for Soprano and Orchestra, *The Wild Winds*, was a setting of Blake's 'Mad Song'. We came to think of these additions as chorales. Blake was a powerful opponent of Newtonian science, and his poetry returns again and again to the perils of divorcing reason from feeling; inseparable from these polarities were the male and female principles which take many forms in his writing. Since I could never aspire to Blake's density of meaning or the simplicity and beauty of his expression, I decided to draw on his strength by quotation and to think of him as the presiding spirit of the piece.

One can only speculate about a world-view that would be entirely consonant with the discoveries of the scientific revolution of this century. It hardly seems possible that what is now orthodox in science should continue for ever to be so much at odds with what we now hold to be commonsense. Objectivity does not exist in quantum mechanics. The observer is a part of what he observes. Reality is changed by the presence of the observer – he can no longer pretend to be invisible. Matter can no longer be thought of as being composed of minute, hard 'bits'; sub-atomic particles are now seen in terms of their tendency to exist, or as fields of energy. The stuff of matter has become the stuff of mind. As one commentator★ has written, 'We are a part of nature, and when we study nature there is no way round the fact that nature is studying itself…' Physics could be regarded as 'the study of the structure of consciousness'. Niels Bohr's Theory of Complementarity – as far as I can grasp it – explains that we do not study the world so much as study our interaction with it. Without us the object of study (light, for example) does not exist. Conversely, without a world to interact with, we do not exist.

Increasingly the talk of physicists has come to sound like theology. Their theories and experiments have caused them to place consciousness at the centre of their concerns, and in many sacred texts they find their new understanding eloquently mirrored or extended. Some physicists are speculating about the ultimate identity of thought and matter. The new physics finds itself in the realm of the ineffable. The supreme intellectual achievement of western civilisation, and its most potent shaping force – science – has perhaps reached a point where it might no longer be at odds with that deep intuitive sense – which seems to have been always with us – that there is a spiritual dimension to our existence, that there is a level of consciousness within us at which a transcendent unity may be perceived and experienced. It would be arrogant of scientists to believe that they might now be able to give some credence to religious experience, or that it is for them to ratify or disprove in their laboratories the teachings of yogis. No one who

★ G. Zukav, *The Dancing Wu Li Masters*, Hutchinson, London, 1979.

takes his or her own thoughts seriously has not asked, in some form or other, Tolstoy's great question: 'Is there any meaning in my life that the inevitable death awaiting me does not destroy?' Previously scientists have claimed that the question lies outside their brief, or have been quick to answer in the negative. Now some physicists are claiming an openness and humility towards religious texts that their predecessors would have found extraordinary.

I believe there are signs that the new physics has begun to be paralleled in many of the ways we study ourselves and our world – the two are no longer so distinct. Whether these emergent signs will ever become dominant, whether they could coalesce into a worldview that could transform our perception of everyday reality, is an open question. To bind intellect to our deepest intuition, to dissolve the sterile division between what is 'out there' and what is 'in here', to grasp that the *Tao*, our science and our art describe the same reality – to be whole – would be to be incapable of devising or dropping a nuclear bomb. How paradoxical that a scientific revolution should now suggest ways in which we might outgrow our materialism and dualism. In the great resurgence of interest in mysticism, eastern philosophies, ancient forms of divination and healing, it would be wrong to see only a fashionable escapism from the orthodoxies of rational scepticism; whether sublimely or inarticulately expressed, this interest represents a sure sense of the limitations of these orthodoxies, and a certainty that not all private experience is explained satisfactorily in materialist terms. Belief in the untapped resources of consciousness is radically reshaping our psychologies and therapies. Holism is a powerful influence too in many fields; holistic medicine and many forms of healing that lie outside the mechanistic approach of conventional medicine stress the consciousness of the practitioner as well as that of the patient, and regard them as interpenetrating. The growing science of ecology places us firmly within the intricate systems of the natural world and warns us that we may yet destroy what sustains us.

One could characterise these two world-views – the Newtonian and that of the new physics – as representing a male and female principle, yang and yin. In the Newtonian universe, there is objectivity; its impartial observer is logical and imagines himself to be all-seeing and invisible; he believes that if he had access to all facts, then everything could be explained. The observer in the Einsteinian universe believes herself to be part of the nature she studies, part of its constant flux; her own consciousness and the surrounding world pervade each other and are interdependent; she knows that at the heart of things there are limitations and paradoxes (the speed of light, the Uncertainty Principle) that prevent her from knowing or expressing everything; she has no illusions of her omniscience, and yet her power is limitless because it does not reside in her alone.

'Shall there be womanly times, or shall we die?' I believe the options to be as stark as that. Could we dare hope that we stand on the threshold of rethinking our world-view so radically that we might confront an evolutionary transformation of consciousness? It may seem a remote possibility, but then it is no more absurd a hope than that we will somehow muddle through. Perhaps less so, for violence is so dominant a feature of our civilisation that failing change it seems unavoidable that sooner or later these weapons – all the power of the new physics at the command of Newtonian ambition – will be fired. Nor is there anything in our recent history to make me believe that in great, compassionate schemes of planning and reorganisation we could engineer social systems that would somehow make nuclear war unthinkable or unnecessary.

Ultimately the change must come within individuals

in sufficient numbers. The dominant theme would have to shift from violence to nurture. Children, not oil or coal or nuclear energy, are our most important resource, and yet we could hardly claim that our culture is organised round their needs. Our education system alone, with its absurd elitism is sufficient demonstration of our betrayal of their potential.

Could we ever learn to 'live lightly on the earth', using the full range of our technological resources, but using them in harmony and balance with our environment rather than in crude violation of it? To desire a given outcome is not sufficient reason for believing it will transpire. If we are free to change, then we are also free to fail. My own belief in the future fluctuates. There are sudden insights into the love and inventiveness of individuals to give me hope for all humankind; and then there are acts of cruelty and destruction that make me despair.

London,
September 1982   I.M.

or
SHALL WE
DIE?

ONE

WOMAN
Midsummer ... midnight.
I left my daughter sleeping and climbed
the hill behind our house to watch the sky.

The bright swarm of the Milky Way.
What stars! What simple joy to see and name them.
I found Orion, Pleiades, the Kids.

A nightjar sang. In the house below
my daughter slept. By her window was a tree.
A fresh wind stirred its leaves. My joy
engulfed the house, the land on which it lay,
the dome of infinite stars.

And even now, as I sit upon the grass,
across the world, in buried places,
sleepless men wait at consoles and watch
the patient sweep of scanners for a sign of penetration,
male virgins, deathmasks in the greenish light.

They and their masters have taken into custody
our lives, all life, my daughter, the nightjar,
the grass beneath my hands.

They and their enemies are men alike;
our enemy is their innocence.

How shall I reconcile this summer's night
with the troubled dreams of all my friends,
with a daughter in a book, dying
in her mother's arms, the dread in every voice?

My daughter, deep love breeds fear of loss.
I look back towards the house.

My heart, and the night's heart, are racing,
as though our world has held its breath
too long, too long.

TWO

CHORUS
On distant stars the laws of mathematics hold.

The velocity of light is constant.

MAN
On countless lonely planets intelligent life
evolves, observes and measures the universe,
questions its beginnings, and discovers at last
by theory and by observation the power
locked in matter that causes suns to burn
for near eternity.

CHORUS
Matter and energy, body and spirit,
the benevolent unity, so simple to intuit,
so difficult to sift.

MAN
On countless planets that power locked in
matter is traced to larger patterns,
the measurements resume in wonder.

But lesser forms, intent on conquest,
helplessly construct the means of their destruction,
and then must face a simple test of wisdom.

CHORUS
Shall we pass, or shall we die?

THREE

MAN
Our load was heavy, the aircraft slow to lift.
The night turned grey, then palest pink.
The unblemished ocean softened in the morning haze.

CHORUS
The aircrew kneels before the priest.
With God's blessing we deliver this bomb.

MAN
Two hundred miles ahead the weather plane
circled our target. We heard its message –
cloud cover less than three-tenths.
At the appointed time we began our ascent.

CHORUS
Our God is manly! In war he refuses us nothing!

MAN
The city below, its river and its tributaries
resembled an outstretched hand.
We shed our burden, our heavy burden,
and turned for home.

CHORUS
Refuses us nothing. Nothing. Nothing.

FOUR

MAN
Our minds are clear of all emotion.

CHORUS
Pure thought alone describes the universe.

MAN
Freely elected, chosen by the people,
we are the makers of laws.

CHORUS
Diligent, logical, disciplined men.

MAN
In our sure hands the security of the State.

CHORUS
The defence of order, freedom, property,
sovereignty, the aspirations of the people.

MAN
Whom we serve.

CHORUS
Whom we lead.

MAN
Secrecy is essential when decisions
weigh heavy on the men of State.
The weak-hearted, the effeminate, the disloyal
must know nothing.

CHORUS
The juries are pricked, the rule of law prevails.

MAN
The enemy incites the traitors in our midst.

CHORUS
Dissidents, extremists, beware!
The rule of law prevails!

FIVE

WOMAN
All night I searched for my daughter.
At dawn a neighbour told me
she had seen her by the river,
among the dead and dying.

I heard her voice calling Mother, Mother,
and I went towards the sound.
My child was completely burned.
The skin had come off her head,
leaving a knot of twisted hair.

My daughter said, Mother, you're late, so late,
please take me back. It hurts, it hurts.
Please take me home. But there were no homes,
no doctors, there was nothing I could do.

I covered up her naked body and held her
in my arms for seven hours.
Late at night she cried out again, Mother,
Mother, and put her arm around my neck,
her small cold arm.

I said, Please say Mother again.
But that was the last time.

CHORUS
When the stars threw down their spears,
And water'd heaven with their tears,
Did He smile His work to see?
Did He who made the Lamb make thee?

SIX

MAN
Two great nations marshal their allies
and prepare for war. Two great nations,
born of revolutions, of compassionate visions
of a world made new, made good
in freedom and in justice.
Not granted by God to Kings,
but made afresh by men.

WOMAN
Is the world redeemed
by shifts of power among the men?

MAN
Here one nation stands jailer to its people's minds,
here the other ransacks the globe, a freedom
sustained by greed. The names of Lenin and Jefferson
are mouthed, the visions are forgotten.
The State appoints its enemies,
bureaucracies propound its simple lies.
The allies, fawning or coerced, take sides.
The cult of weaponry taints every mind,
derides compassion, distorts all relation.

War is urged by governments in the name of the people.

WOMAN
Shall we always be fooled by these ancient lies?
Who is my enemy? Who is the enemy of my child?

CHORUS
We shall crush you lest we shall be crushed.

SEVEN

WOMAN
Midsummer ... two hours before dawn,
in the house below my husband and daughter sleep.
The stars fade, the moon has risen,
derided womanly moon who longs to be
our emblem in this manly world.

Grieving moon, do our virile times
suggest to you the metaphor of rape,
the conquest of nature, the slaughter of species,
the burning of forests, the poisoning of ocean and air,
the tyranny of scale, the weapons, the weapons.

MAN AND WOMAN
Our science mocks magic and the human heart,
our knowledge is the brutal mastery of the unknown.

CHORUS
Cruelty has a human heart,
And jealousy a human face;
Terror the human form divine,
And secrecy the human dress.

The human dress is forged iron,
The human form a fiery forge,
The human face a furnace sealed,
The human heart its hungry gorge.

WOMAN
Shall there be womanly times, or shall we die?
Are there men unafraid of gentleness?

Can we have strength without aggression,
without disgust,
strength to bind feeling to the intellect?

MAN AND WOMAN
The planet does not turn for us alone.
Science is a form of wonder, knowledge a form of love.
Are we too late to love ourselves?
Shall we change, or shall we die?

WOMAN
The moon lifts higher and brightens.
Only shadows point the way.

CHORUS
For Mercy has a human heart,
Pity a human face,
And Love, the human form divine,
And Peace, the human dress.

Then every man, of every clime,
That prays in his distress,
Prays to the human form divine,
Love, Mercy, Pity, Peace.